MARVIN
COMPOSES
A TEA

MARVIN COMPOSES A TEA

AND OTHER HUMOROUS STORIES
Compiled by the Editors
of
Highlights for Children

BOYDS MILLS PRESS

Compilation copyright © 1992 by Boyds Mills Press, Inc.
Contents copyright by Highlights for Children, Inc.
Published by Boyds Mills Press, Inc.
A Highlights Company
815 Church Street
Honesdale, Pennsylvania 18431
Printed in the United States of America
Publisher Cataloging-in-Publication Data
Main entry under title.
    Marvin composes a tea : humorous stories from Highlights / compiled
by the Editors of Highlights for Children.
[96] p. : ill. ;   cm.
Stories originally published in Highlights for Children.
Summary: A collection of humorous stories for young people.
ISBN 1-878093-40-1
[1. Humorous stories] I. Highlights for Children. II. Title.
                              [F]   1992
Library of Congress Catalog Card Number: 90-85916

Drawings by Judith Hunt and Carlos Garzón
Distributed by St. Martin's Press

    4 5 6 7 8 9 10

Highlights® is a registered trademark of Highlights for Children, Inc.

CONTENTS

Marvin Composes a Tea by Pam Hopper 7

Dudwilley, the Yum-Yum Dog
by Elaine Pageler 13

Get Back Here, Loretta! by Melanie Vickers........21

For Sale: One Mom
by Kathy Overholser Kalmar 27

The Wizard's Sneeze by D. L. Halterman 33

Fabulous Lily LaGrande by Eileen Spinelli 39

Mr. Bizbee and Miss Doolittle
by Tina Tibbitts 47

The Peanut-Butter-Cookie Kid
by Janette Gentry 53

Whackytack Construction Company
by Lynn Hartsell 59

Pamela's Parrot by Betty Bates 67

The Legend of Pumpkin Hollow
by Laura Mellen 73

Francis Milliken Minds His Manners
by Joyce Durham Barrett 79

A Simply Monstrous Time by Linda Neves 85

The Backward Runner by Elaine Wilson 91

Marvin Composes a Tea

By Pam Hopper

Marvin Sludge is a composer, which means he writes music. He spends a lot of time practicing sounds on different instruments.

Not everyone appreciates Marvin's composing. Not his teacher, who would rather he learn to multiply his fractions. Not his mother, who'd rather he learn to turn his socks right-side-out. And especially not Marvin's next-door neighbor,

Mrs. Pasquini. She convinced the other tenants in his building to sign a letter to ban Marvin's composing.

One day, while Marvin was playing the piccolo to see if a *dee-diddle-dee* was just the right sound to finish his new concerto, there was a knock on his door. He was quite surprised to see all of the apartment house tenants.

"Good afternoon, everyone," Marvin said with a smile. "What can I do for you?"

"We've come about your composing, Marvin."

"Ah, you're probably wondering what I'm working on, aren't you, Mrs. Pasquini? If you step into my apartment, perhaps I can play part of my new concerto for you." Marvin motioned for everyone to come in, and, not knowing what else to do, they did.

"Please sit down, and I'll get some tea and fig bars for all of us. I'm so glad you decided to visit."

This wasn't what everyone expected. They had planned to give Marvin their letter of complaint and go home. Marvin returned with a tray full of fig bars and teacups. "Tea, Miss Wentworth?"

She nodded. "What were you playing before we knocked, Marvin?" she asked.

"That was the piccolo. I'm trying to find just the right sound for my new concerto, but I'm afraid I haven't found it yet."

"It must be difficult composing music," said Mr. Antonio, reaching for a fig bar.

"Which brings me to why we are here," interrupted Mrs. Pasquini.

"Ah, yes," said Marvin. "You wanted to hear the concerto I'm working on, didn't you?"

Before Mrs. Pasquini could say anything, Marvin began playing his concerto, using all his different instruments. When he finished, everyone clapped except Mrs. Pasquini.

"I often hear you composing," Mr. Freebie said, "and I must say I like the part where the trombone goes *bwah-bwah hmm bwah-bwah hmm bwah-bwah hmm bwah*."

"Why, thank you, Mr. Freebie. I'm rather embarrassed that you can hear me playing. Does it bother anyone? I certainly wouldn't want to bother any of my neighbors."

Mr. Antonio cleared his throat slightly and remarked, "Well, my parakeet *did* faint one day. Nothing serious, but it was a little alarming to see poor Polly flat on her feathers like that. I think the part where the bass drum went *ba-boom boom ba-boom ba* frightened her."

"My dishes *do* rattle sometimes, but no harm is really done, and it keeps the dust off them," Miss Wentworth said, giggling.

"Well, Marvin, I must admit Fifi *does* howl

when you play the violin, but I'm sure she's just singing," added Mrs. Oliver-Hollisday.

"I rather like the violin part, too, Mrs. Oliver-Hollisday. Does it really bother poor Fifi's ears?" asked Miss Wentworth.

"I'm afraid it does, Miss Wentworth. I *do* enjoy violins. They make such lovely sounds. Don't you think so?"

Miss Wentworth agreed, and then everyone began discussing their favorite instrument and why fig bars went so well with tea. In fact, everyone began talking to everyone else, something they rarely did.

Everyone was having a delightful time except Mrs. Pasquini, who looked quite cross.

"Marvin, there is something I think you need to know . . ." But as she started to stand up, the long feather on Mrs. Oliver-Hollisday's hat tickled her right on the nose and made her sneeze, which startled Mr. Freebie into hiccuping, which made Miss Wentworth giggle, which caused Mr. Antonio to laugh. Soon everyone was laughing.

Their laughter sounded like this: *hee hee giggle-giggle haw haw hoo snicker giggle-titter hee hee hoo.*

"Wonderful!" Marvin exclaimed. "Bravo, everybody!"

They all stopped laughing and looked at him.

"That's just the sound I've been looking for! Laughter is the best music I know. I don't think I could capture it as well on any of my instruments. Would you mind performing with me next Saturday when I present my new concerto?"

No one knew what to say. And then Miss Wentworth said she wouldn't mind. Mr. Freebie said it would be his pleasure. Mr. Antonio thought it was a splendid idea, and Mrs. Oliver-Hollisday said she would be delighted. Everyone agreed to perform. Everyone, that is, except Mrs. Pasquini, who stood up with her complaint letter in her hand.

"Marvin, before we go any further, there is something I need to do first." All eyes were on her as she held up the complaint letter. "There is just one thing I have to say. We don't need this letter at all." And with that she tore the letter into teeny-tiny pieces. "Laughter is certainly music to my ears. I haven't laughed in years. I would love to contribute my giggles to your concerto, too."

Everyone clapped, and someone asked if there was any tea left, while someone else asked if there were any more fig bars. And soon they were all talking and laughing once again.

Dudwilley, the Yum-Yum Dog

By Elaine Pageler

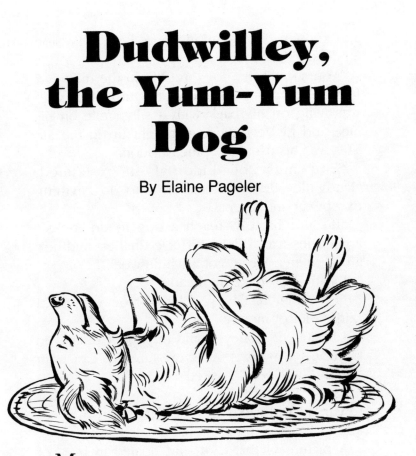

My friend Jessica first saw the ad in the paper. "Look, Angie, here's a way to make money," she said, waving the *Green Hills News* under my nose. She read me an ad in the Help Wanted column: "Dog wanted for Yum-Yum Dog Biscuits commercial. Must be well trained and know tricks. Auditions to be held at Preston Studios, 1 P.M. Saturday."

"You supply the dog, and I'll do the training," Jessica went on. I glanced at Dudwilley, who was lying on his back with a silly smile on his face and his feet sticking straight up in the air. This was his usual sleeping position.

"You must be kidding!" I exclaimed. "Dudwilley doesn't know how to do anything except eat and sleep."

"It's not hard to teach a dog to do tricks," argued Jessica. "I helped Uncle Charles, and he's a dog trainer. We've got a whole week."

I started to shake my head.

"TV commercials pay a lot of money," Jessica said, "a lot of money."

I hesitated. Money would buy the jean skirt in Gordon's window. "Are you sure we can train him in one week?" I asked.

"Sure! All we need are dog biscuits for rewards, and we'll have Dudwilley doing all kinds of tricks," Jessica replied.

A picture of that jean skirt floated in front of my eyes. "I guess I could use my allowance to buy some Yum-Yums," I decided.

The next afternoon we tried to teach Dudwilley to fetch. It was a hard trick for him to learn. Both Jessica and I got sore arms throwing sticks. Dudwilley refused to understand that he should bring them back to earn a reward.

Finally Jessica said, "Oh, give him a few Yum-Yums anyway. We'll continue his training tomorrow."

By the end of the week Dudwilley had learned only three tricks, and most of our Yum-Yums were gone.

"Angie," Mom called as I came downstairs for breakfast on Saturday morning, "what are those dog biscuit boxes doing in your room?"

"Maybe she eats dog biscuits for snacks," said my brother, Alec.

"Very funny!" I snapped. "For your information, Jessica and I are training Dudwilley for a Yum-Yum Dog Biscuits commercial."

"Our Dudwilley?" whooped Alec.

"Yes, our Dudwilley! Jessica knows all about training dogs!"

"And I know all about Dudwilley," my brother said with a giggle. "Look at him. All he knows how to do is eat and sleep."

Dudwilley was lying in the middle of the rug

with that grin on his face and his feet straight up in the air. Loud snores rumbled from his direction.

"I'm afraid Alec is right," said Mom. "It's hard to teach an old dog new tricks."

Before I could say anything, Jessica crashed through the door. "Come on, Angie!" she called. "We only have a few hours to finish training Dudwilley. He needs to know more tricks."

We took Dudwilley out to the backyard and worked all morning. By noon he hadn't learned anything new and even seemed to have forgotten his old tricks. We had just enough time to dash to Preston Studios.

The audition room was filled with dogs and people. It was exciting to everyone but Dudwilley, who looked tired. He dropped on the floor and started to roll over onto his back.

"Get him on his feet!" commanded Jessica. "We can't let anyone see the silly way he sleeps!"

"Listen, everybody," called the audition director. "We will do a videotape of each dog doing his tricks. Remember, only the dog may be onstage. Trainers must call their directions from the side. There will be a big bowl of Yum-Yums on the stage for each dog to eat when he finishes."

Jessica and I watched, with Dudwilley squeezed between us. It was the only way to keep him on his feet. All of the dogs were good. They seemed to know every trick in the world.

We were the very last act. I led Dudwilley to the middle of the stage, unfastened his leash, and headed for the sidelines. Then Jessica gave him his first command. "Speak!" she called.

But Dudwilley just stood there blinking up at the bright lights.

"Tell him to beg," I whispered. "He's better at that."

Jessica kept calling commands. Finally, Dudwilley got the idea he was supposed to do something. He looked around and spotted the bowl of Yum-Yums.

"No, not yet!" shouted Jessica.

It was too late. Dudwilley raced over to the Yum-Yums, wolfed them down, and threw himself on the floor. Within seconds, he was fast asleep with his feet straight up in the air and a silly grin on his face.

The crowd roared.

"Oh, no!" we groaned.

"Wonderful!" shouted the audition director.

"Yes," called the writer. "We must have Dudwilley, the happy dog who dreams of Yum-Yum Dog Biscuits."

Dudwilley was given a contract, a year's supply of dog biscuits, and a lot of money. I got the jean skirt at Gordon's, and Jessica got a new sweater. Best of all, she and I have become official dog trainers. All the other kids want us to teach their dogs how to sleep on their backs with their feet in the air and grin just like Dudwilley, the famous Yum-Yum dog.

Get Back Here, Loretta!

By Melanie Vickers

I, Jinks Lepley, have a two-year-old sister named Loretta. I'm going to tell you what life with a little sister is like, and I won't leave out the worst parts.

Just yesterday morning Mom announced we were going shopping to find Dad a birthday present. I ran to my room and got out all the money I had in the world—$3.75. I poked the money down to the bottom of my pocket and ran into the living room. "Ready," I said.

"Hold it, Jinks," Mom said. "Loretta has to take a morning nap."

Loretta was sitting in her highchair with cereal stuck in her hair. She laughed out loud, as if someone had just told an elephant joke.

To kill time, I collected night crawlers, hung upside down in the sycamore tree, did cartwheels into the house, and then did forward rolls under the kitchen table. "Time to go, Jinks," Mom said, peeking down at me. I jumped up and bumped the top of my head on the bottom of the table. I took my money out to count it again. There was only three dollars. Seventy-five cents down the tubes!

At the mall Mom got out the stroller for Loretta and gave me the honor of pushing her. Right off, Loretta yelled, "Zat? Zat?" In baby language that means "What's that?" Believe it or not, my mom answers her every time she asks it.

First we stopped in the pet shop. Up front was a box with a marshmallow-colored puppy in it. I asked the clerk how much the dog cost, and he said, "Two fifty."

"I'll take him," I said. "I have three dollars. Dad will love him!"

"Oh, no," the man said, sounding like he was trying not to laugh. "He's two hundred and fifty dollars."

On the way out, Loretta threw her box of animal crackers to the puppy, and he gobbled them up, paper and all.

Then Mom stopped in front of a store that had big signs saying SALE. "Jinks, you push Loretta around while I look. I'll only be a minute."

It never fails. As soon as Mom is out of sight, Loretta goes bananas. She started waving her arms and yelling "Mum! Mum!" She tried to stand up in her stroller, only it turned over on top of her. What a racket! I got her back in and pushed her to the other side of the mall.

In front of us was a magic stand. The guy in the booth made a white rope turn red. Dad always loves magic tricks. "I'll take it," I said, pulling out a dollar bill. But, before I could hand it to him, I looked down and saw that the stroller was empty. Now I was the one waving my arms and yelling. "Get back here, Loretta!"

Across the hall I saw the ruffles on the back of Loretta's plastic pants. Have you ever tried to catch a bowling ball moving at top speed? I grabbed her from behind and carried her back to the stroller. Where was my dollar? I looked everywhere we had been, but it was gone.

Mom called us over to the counter. "Jinks,"

she said, "I need one more dollar for Dad's present. Can you lend me one of yours?" I gave her a dollar, and she patted me on the hand, not noticing the teeth marks where Loretta had bitten me. How was I going to explain about not having a present for Dad?

On the way out of the mall we passed a photo booth, and I asked Mom to wait. Here was my last chance to get Dad a birthday present.

Inside, I closed the curtain and sat on the little stool that twirls around. Just as I put my money in the slot, Loretta's head popped up under the curtain.

"See BeBe," she hollered. Then she jumped like a frog and landed in my lap just as the camera clicked.

"No, Loretta," Mom called, reaching in to get her, and the camera clicked again.

Clamping her arms around my neck, Loretta squealed "Inks!" and planted a wet kiss on my cheek. Mom and I looked at each other as if we had just seen King Kong. The camera clicked for the last picture.

"Did you hear what she said?" Mom asked.

I was smiling. Loretta had never said my name before. "Inks, Inks, Inks," she said over and over and all the way home.

Those were some of the craziest pictures I've ever seen. It looked like Mom and Loretta and I had decided to get in that little booth and have a wrestling match.

At home I glued the pictures on paper and decorated the edges with seashells and glitter. Dad said it was his favorite present.

Now, instead of wearing out my eardrums with "Zat? Zat?" Loretta says "Inks" a million times a day. I can live with that.

For Sale: One Mom

By Kathy Overholser Kalmar

Hi. I'm Mandy, my brother's name is Vic, and this is my family's story.

The day our mom quit being a regular mom was the beginning of our problem.

All mothers are problems, forever telling you to wear boots in the snow, take an umbrella, pick up your clothes. It's the way mothers are.

But our problem was much worse.

We had already lived through the Working Mom routine. Since our mom was a teacher, that wasn't as easy as it sounds. But things got worse when she became a writer.

At first we were happy, because everyone knows that writers work at home. She'd have plenty of time to bake those homemade chocolate chip cookies, we thought, and we'd get an ordinary mom again.

Only that's not how it went.

Mom said writers don't make enough money, so she still needed to teach. She got even busier than before. Whenever we asked her about something, she always said, "Ssh! Can't you see I'm writing?" We looked and looked, but we couldn't see any writing. The paper was blank! I guess writers do a lot of thinking before they begin writing.

When we asked simple questions like "When's dinner?" Mom would say, "Ssh! Dinner is at dinnertime," and go back to writing. We learned that dinner started when the typing stopped, unless Mom tried doing both things at once. If she wrote while she cooked, dinner bit the dust. She forgot about it until the smoke alarm reminded her. Not only was dinner ruined, but so were our eardrums. Smoke alarms are loud!

It wasn't long before Mom's writing started embarrassing me and Vic. She started to write about us! Sure, she changed our names, but you could still tell it was us. Nobody is safe around a Writer Mom.

One day at the supermarket, Mom grabbed my arm and scared the daylights out of me while we waited in the check-out line. "Quick! Quick! I need some paper! Where's your pen?" she asked. The next thing I knew, she grabbed a grocery bag and started scribbling on it. She held up the whole check-out line!

"Story idea," she said to the check-out girl, who looked at Mom like she was goofy.

Another time Mom got a story idea at a restaurant. She wrote on every piece of paper on

the table. She even wrote on our napkins and place mats! Can you imagine how it looked when the waitress saw Mom putting the place mats and napkins into her purse?

Vic and I had to do something about Mom. We were getting desperate. That's when our friend Cindy suggested that we put our mom up for sale. It turns out she'd heard about a "Rent-A-Granny" company on TV and figured we could try the same thing.

"Wait a minute!" I cried. "She's our mom!"

"The worst that could happen," Cindy said, "is that she'll see how miserable you are and stop writing about you and start baking again. And isn't that what you really want her to do?"

That night we started writing our ad to sell Mom, listing all of the best things about her. It's not easy trying to sell your own mother, but the ad sounded pretty good.

For Sale: One Mom. Makes yummy chocolate chip cookies. Loves children. Has her own interests and lets you have yours, too. Good listener, great hugger, sometimes even lets you eat fast food. Friendly and pretty. Doesn't yell, and makes you part of her work. Lets you have more than one friend in the house at a time. Worth her weight in gold!

Vic looked at me, and I looked at him.

"Best mom in the world," Vic said.

"Writes great stories about us," I added.

Vic crumpled up the ad. Although Mom still writes in her notebooks and embarrasses us, there's nobody like her.

Then a really surprising thing happened! I decided to write a story about my mom. The title is "For Sale: One Mom." Mom sent it to a magazine just for kids, and they printed it! My mom, the writer, says writing must run in our family.

Vic says two writers in the family are too much! He's writing another ad.

For Sale: One Mom and One Big Sister . . .

The Wizard's Sneeze

By D. L. Halterman

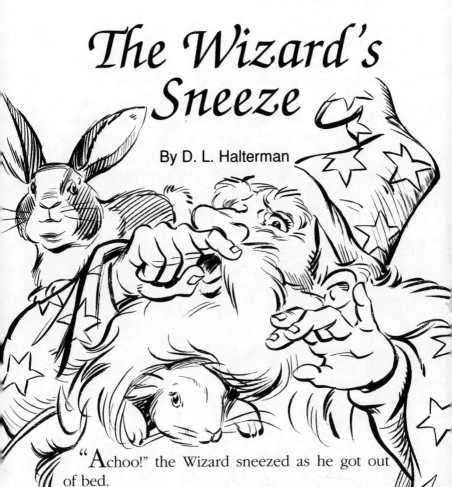

"Achoo!" the Wizard sneezed as he got out of bed.

"Oh, no!" he cried when his slippers turned into small white rabbits hopping about the room.

Trying not to sneeze again, the Wizard held

his breath until his face turned a bright cherry red—"Achoo!"

Four more rabbits hopped out from under the bed. Two were white, and two were gray. With one finger held tightly under his nose so he wouldn't sneeze again, the Wizard slipped into his robe. Quickly he padded across the cold floor of the castle and into the kitchen, where his wife was having breakfast.

Behind him came the rabbits, skipping along like so many fluffy clouds on a windy day. "Not again!" the Wizard's wife shouted when she saw him standing there, nervously holding a finger under his nose while the rabbits played around his bare feet.

"I'm afraid so," the Wizard admitted, and . . .
"Achoo!" he sneezed again.

This time eight more rabbits magically
appeared all over the kitchen. "Keep your finger
under your nose!" his wife shouted as she
wagged her own finger at him.

"I am, I am," the Wizard said, trying to hold
back a sneeze. His nose tingled like the fizz
from soda pop.

"I remember the last time this happened. We
were up to our chins in rabbits before you could
say *hop, skip,* and *jump,*" his wife said.

"It *was* sort of funny, wasn't it?" the Wizard
mumbled. With his finger still under his nose, he
sounded as if he had his head in a bucket. He

scratched his nose, and . . . "Achoo!" he sneezed again.

Sixteen more rabbits popped out of everywhere. One of them was sitting on top of his wife's head like a new bonnet. The Wizard giggled, and . . . "Achoo!" he sneezed again.

"It's not funny!" his wife said, removing the rabbit from her head and the two that suddenly appeared on the table. "Remember what the King said he would do if this happened again," she warned.

"I do. I do." The Wizard laughed, and . . . "Achoo!" he sneezed again.

Now there were rabbits everywhere. Big rabbits, little rabbits. Long and short rabbits. White, gray, brown, all colors of rabbits—even one that matched the bright blue eyes of the Wizard.

The Wizard couldn't stop laughing—or sneezing. He sneezed and sneezed. And the rabbits kept coming, faster and faster, until they almost reached the top of the table.

Then—as suddenly as it had started—it stopped!

No more sneezing.

No more rabbits!

"I think it's over," the Wizard said cautiously when he could get his breath at last.

"You may be right," his wife said hopefully.

She brushed a bright orange rabbit off her lap.

"Hiccup!" went the Wizard.

"Oh, no!" screamed his wife as a large green bumpy frog poked its head from her cereal bowl.

"Gribbit," said the frog.

"Hiccup!" went the Wizard again.

Fabulous Lily LaGrande

By Eileen Spinelli

Maggie Winkler was so excited she could almost feel her freckles twitter. The fabulous movie star—none other than Lily LaGrande— was coming to dinner. In only two weeks!

"We don't believe you," said all her friends at school.

But it was true. Lily LaGrande was touring college campuses across the country. Maggie's father happened to teach mathematics at one of those colleges—Franklin C. Hart. It was only right that Miss LaGrande be invited to someone's home to freshen up before her appearance. And, of course, she had to be fed.

The entire Franklin C. Hart staff wanted to freshen and feed the gorgeous Lily LaGrande. So they all put their names in a hat, crossed their fingers, made their wishes, and held their breath. And the name that came out of the hat was Ralph Winkler.

"Bravo!" The English professor beamed and slapped Maggie's father on the back.

"Oo-la-laaaa!" whispered the French professor, smacking his lips against his fingertips.

"We'll clean the house from top to bottom," Maggie's mother announced when she heard the news. And that's what they did. The Winklers scrubbed floors, shampooed rugs, and shined windows. They painted the guest room a lovely shade of pink and covered the guest bed with their very best quilt. They washed their best china. When they were done, the house sparkled.

"Don't tell a soul Miss LaGrande is coming here," cautioned Mr. Winkler. "We want her to enjoy her privacy."

Maggie blushed. "I told all the girls at school."

"Ay-yi-yi," said Mr. Winkler with a sigh.

"It's okay," said Maggie. "No one believed me."

When the big day came and the Winklers gathered at the living room window, it was obvious that they were not only as clean as the china—they were changed. Mrs. Winkler had lost seven pounds. Mr. Winkler had grown a mustache. And Maggie had traded her jeans for a pale lavender dress. She was waiting to present the enchanting Lily LaGrande with a bouquet of roses.

They waited and waited. At last a car pulled up. It was the longest, bluest car Maggie had ever seen.

"There she is!" cried Mr. Winkler.

"Hurry, hurry," coaxed Maggie, who was the first one out.

"Calm down," cautioned Mrs. Winkler.

A tall man in a fancy uniform opened the door of the big car. Out stepped the magnificent Lily LaGrande. She oozed fur and gold and glitter. "Where *is* everyone?" she inquired, sniffing the air.

"Everyone?" said Mrs. Winkler.

The stately Miss LaGrande fluttered her long red fingernails, first to the right, then to the left. "Everyone! The band! The press! My fans!"

Maggie's father gulped. "Oh, yes. Yes indeed." And off he ran down the street, banging on doors.

Within minutes Mr. Franconi was standing on the sidewalk playing "Yankee Doodle Dandy" on his harmonica. Mrs. Ogilvie, who published the local recipe newsletter, arrived with pad and pencil. Five-year-old Hermy Rachett asked the fantastic Miss LaGrande if she would autograph his T-shirt.

"Well—I never!" swooned the majestic Lily LaGrande, and, brushing the neighbors aside, she waltzed into the house.

Maggie caught up with her. "These are for you," she said, smiling and extending the rose bouquet.

The exotic Miss LaGrande's powdered, peerless nose twitched. Her red mouth flew open. "Aaahhh-CHOO! Get those away from me!" she shrieked. "I'm allergic to ro-ro-ooh-ahh-AAAHHHCHOO!" And, with that, her long, dark, wonderful wig shot across the room and landed in the punch.

Mrs. Winkler stepped forward. "Perhaps you'd like to freshen up."

By the time the stunning Miss LaGrande's wig was washed and dried, it looked more like a mop than a wig.

"Oh, boohoo, boohoo!" she cried.

Mr. Winkler offered his handkerchief. "Perhaps you'd like to blow your nose."

The glamorous Miss LaGrande blew so hard and so loud that she popped four buttons.

"I'll get my sewing kit," said Mrs. Winkler.

Finally the elegant Miss LaGrande was back together. Maggie suggested a tour of the house.

"Good idea," said Mr. Winkler, nervously tugging at his new mustache.

They took the exciting Miss LaGrande through the kitchen, where pots bubbled merrily on the stove. They took her through the dining room, where the table was set with their finest, cleanest china. Then they went upstairs.

"This is the guest room," said Mr. Winkler.

Unfortunately, Maggie had forgotten to put away the paint can. Even more unfortunately, the incredible Miss LaGrande was so busy batting her false eyelashes that she didn't see it.

Pip-tip Ka-BOOMBAH! Lily LaGrande tripped. Her high heels flew off, and she herself tumbled wig-first into the bed.

Mrs. Winkler plumped the pillow. "Perhaps you'd like to take a nap before dinner."

At 6 P.M. Maggie delicately woke the splendid, snoring Lily LaGrande. "Dinner is ready."

Mr. Winkler, Maggie, and Miss LaGrande sat at the dining room table while Mrs. Winkler went to the kitchen for the roast beef. She opened the oven door, and a cloud of smoke billowed out.

"Oh dear, the roast is burning!"

"I'll call the fire department!" yelled Maggie.

"Cough, cough, cough!" went the delightful Miss LaGrande.

Mr. Winkler took the movie star's arm and led her away. "Perhaps you'd like a bit of fresh air." Bravely, Mr. Winkler led the way through the smoking house. He threw open the front door and gallantly stepped aside. The dazzling Lily LaGrande was just in time to catch the fire fighters spraying their powerful hoses.

Mrs. Winkler emerged from the smoke. "Perhaps you'd like to borrow my umbrella."

When the fire department left, Mr. Winkler looked at his watch. "It's time I took Miss LaGrande to the college for her appearance."

"I'll get her coat," offered Maggie.

Maggie pulled the luxurious fur from the closet. Out flew eighteen well-fed moths. The coat now looked more like a fishing net than fur.

Mrs. Winkler grabbed her orange bowling jacket. "Perhaps this will keep you just as warm."

Outside in the driveway, Mr. Winkler was trying to start his car. At first it made a whining, mournful sound, then no sound at all. "The battery's dead," sobbed Mr. Winkler, his head

buried against the steering wheel.

Maggie ran to get her bike. "The tire's flat," she moaned.

Mrs. Winkler came running from the shed. "The wheelbarrow works!"

Mr. Winkler helped the incomparable Lily LaGrande into the wheelbarrow. "I'll get you there in no time," he vowed, pushing the movie star down the driveway and onto the road.

"Good-bye, Miss LaGrande!" called Mrs. Winkler. "It was so nice to meet you."

Maggie waved excitedly. "I hope you'll come visit us again sometime soon!"

Mr. Bizbee
and
Miss Doolittle

By Tina Tibbitts

Mr. Bizbee lived in the tidiest house in town. The grass around it was always trimmed. Even the flowers stood up straight in their beds. Mr. Bizbee would not have had it any other way.

One day someone moved into the empty house next door. Mr. Bizbee decided to go over and say hello.

47

"I'm Miss Doolittle," said the new neighbor. "And this is my cat, Snoozy."

"May I help you unpack your boxes?" asked Mr. Bizbee.

"No, thanks," Miss Doolittle replied. "Whenever I need something, I'll unpack it."

"Perhaps I could mow your lawn," offered Mr. Bizbee.

"Mowing the lawn is a waste of time," replied Miss Doolittle. "Besides, long grass and wildflowers are pretty."

After that, Mr. Bizbee did not go over to talk to Miss Doolittle. They clearly did not think alike. Soon they began to irk one another.

Blooming in Miss Doolittle's yard were what

Mr. Bizbee called weeds. The wind blew their seeds into Mr. Bizbee's yard. Then he had a bumper crop of weeds. He sweated for hours, pulling them up while Miss Doolittle sat in her yard admiring the butterflies.

One day Mr. Bizbee put freshly baked bread out on the porch to cool. Miss Doolittle's cat, Snoozy, jumped up on the table and curled up between the warm loaves of bread. When Mr. Bizbee saw this, he grabbed Snoozy and took him over to Miss Doolittle. He told her that cat hairs were all over his wonderful bread. She replied that he never should have left the bread out where Snoozy could get near it.

A month later, as Miss Doolittle unpacked a box to get out the mop, she found her old tuba. She began tooting it every day with the windows of her house open. Mr. Bizbee wore earmuffs to shut out the noise.

Then Mr. Bizbee began learning French. Every evening he sat on his back porch listening to his French records. The records said the same words over and over. Miss Doolittle got tired of hearing the records and went out to tell him so. Mr. Bizbee said something. Miss Doolittle didn't understand French, but it sounded rude to her. She stomped into her house, slamming the door.

Things did not change until one afternoon in autumn. Mr. Bizbee was putting candles on his birthday cake. He felt silly having it by himself, but he had forgotten to invite anyone over. And it was too late now.

Suddenly he heard Miss Doolittle playing "Happy Birthday" on her tuba. Mr. Bizbee could hardly believe his ears. How could she know about his birthday? Although she had strange ideas, Miss Doolittle might yet perhaps be a kind person. Mr. Bizbee decided to go over and share his cake with her.

When Miss Doolittle opened her door, she nearly dropped her tuba. There stood Mr. Bizbee holding a birthday cake with candles blazing. Too surprised to speak, she waved him inside.

"First, Miss Doolittle, let me thank you for cheering me up by playing 'Happy Birthday' on your tuba," said Mr. Bizbee.

"I didn't think you liked my tuba playing," replied Miss Doolittle. "And thank you for making me a birthday cake! How did you ever know?"

Mr. Bizbee stared at her. "I made the cake for my birthday," he said.

"And I played 'Happy Birthday' to myself on the tuba," said Miss Doolittle.

Then they both had a good laugh.

"Do you like chocolate cake?" asked Mr. Bizbee, still chuckling.

"It's my favorite kind," replied Miss Doolittle.

So together they had a double birthday party. Even Snoozy joined the fun.

And since that special birthday, Mr. Bizbee and Miss Doolittle have never let their different ways of thinking keep them from being friends.

The Peanut-Butter-Cookie Kid

By Janette Gentry

"Buzzy Beecher! Go away!" Mitzi howled at her little brother. Mitzi was lying flat on her stomach, hanging on to Lester, her squirming, squealing white pig.

"Don't think Lester likes corn," Buzzy said, taking a big bite out of a peanut butter cookie.

"You're scaring him!" yelled Mitzi. "He goes berserk every time he sees you. Go somewhere else!"

Buzzy crammed the rest of the crunchy cookie in his mouth. His cheeks puffed like a chipmunk's. "I wink Wester wikes—" he mumbled through the mouthful of cookie.

"Eeeeeeeeee," squealed Lester.

"Scoot!" yelled Mitzi.

"Well, okay," Buzzy said. He went toward the house.

Mitzi sat up, gripping Lester in her arms. "Now, now," she murmured. "Buzzy is gone." She scratched the pig's stomach. Lester gave a satisfied grunt and relaxed.

"You don't want Grubby to win the race, do you?" Mitzi asked the pig.

"Huh," grunted Lester.

"You can win, Lester. Just keep your mind on your business. And forget Buzzy."

Mitzi got up and carried Lester to a narrow pen near the barn. At one end of the pen, a loose cardboard flap hung over a square opening. Mitzi climbed into the pen and put Lester down. "Let's go over it one more time, champ," she said. "When I clap my hands, you zoom out of here. Remember—delicious, nutritious corn, only twenty meters away. Straight ahead."

Lester yawned and grunted something that sounded like "Ug."

"All right. Ready, get set . . . ." Mitzi smacked her hands together close to Lester's ear. "Go!"

Like a flash, Lester went through the flap. He didn't even blink at the pile of corn. He was a white blur, zipping across the field to the house.

Mitzi caught him at the back steps, where Buzzy sat munching on another peanut butter cookie. "Might as well give up," Mitzi said in disgust.

"I think—" Buzzy began.

"I know," Mitzi interrupted. "You think Lester hates corn."

The next day Buzzy watched Mitzi and Lester from the door of the hayloft. The training went better. Lester was very calm.

"You're a winner, champ. I feel it in my bones," Mitzi told him.

But the feeling in Mitzi's bones changed when she arrived at the fair the next morning. There were twelve other pigs in the race, all bigger than Lester. And Lester was number thirteen.

Grubby was in the pen next to Lester's. He snuffed and snorted angrily, looking through the slats at Lester. He seemed to have his greedy eyes on the pile of corn already. Grubby's owner sneered at Mitzi. "Ol' Lester looks mighty weak and pale."

Mitzi didn't answer. When she fastened the banner with the number thirteen on it around Lester's middle, she whispered, "You show him, champ."

Then the loudspeaker was blaring, "Come one, come all. The pig race is about to begin."

"Ready, boys and girls?" the referee called. "Get set!" Then there was the loud crack of the starting gun.

Lester pushed the flap up with his snout and peered out. All the other pigs rushed out of their pens. They began to mill around, squealing and snorting. All but Grubby. He was headed in the right direction.

"Go, Lester," Mitzi begged.

"Huh," grunted Lester. He withdrew his snout and turned around. And, as if to say "Watch this," he backed slowly through the flap.

And then Mitzi saw Buzzy standing at the fence in a direct line with the pile of corn. "Oh, nooooooo," Mitzi groaned loudly. "If Lester sees Buzzy . . ."

Suddenly, with a loud squeal, Lester whirled around. He sniffed the air, gave a springy bounce, and was off!

Mitzi couldn't watch. She covered her eyes with her hands. Through her fingers she saw Lester sideswipe Grubby and plow right through the corn pile, scattering it everywhere. Then

Lester was at the fence, doing a little dance—right in front of Buzzy.

Mitzi got to Lester just in time to see Buzzy poke a cookie through the wire. Lester gulped it down.

"Lester likes cookies," Buzzy said.

Mitzi laughed. "Boy! How could I be so dumb? Peanut butter cookies. That's what Lester wanted all the time."

"Yep," said Buzzy.

"And I wouldn't listen to you."

"Nope," said Buzzy.

There was laughing and clapping and cheering as the judge came over to hand Mitzi a shiny trophy with a silver pig on top. "Would you like to say anything, Mitzi?" the judge asked.

"Yes, sir." Mitzi grinned. "I want to thank my brother for helping Lester win. His name is Buzzy, but I call him the Peanut-Butter-Cookie Kid."

"Yep," said Buzzy. And he poked another cookie through the wire to Lester.

Whackytack Construction Company

By Lynn Hartsell

Wham! Bang! Slam! Freddie Lightheart is busy building a house. Freddie is a good carpenter—just noisy. Every fifth nail bends over, but the rest go in straight.

His partner, Sam Goodsaw, is even better. All his nails go in straight. Sam is quiet and neat and never hits his thumb with his hammer.

Together they own the Whackytack

Construction Company. Freddie thought up the name. Sam thought it was silly, but people do remember it when they want a fence built around their new dog, or a bedroom added on or taken off.

Each has a truck with the Whackytack name painted on its side. Sam's truck is small and white and always runs. Freddie's truck is blue in some places, green in others, and rusty in between. It is big enough to go to the lumberyard and not get hidden behind piles of wood.

Sam always wears a clean carpenter's apron. It has big pockets to hold nails, a special loop for his hammer, and a small pocket for his little plane. Anytime a board doesn't fit "just so," Sam takes that plane out and shaves down the edges until it fits perfectly. He is very particular. (Freddie says he is "picky.") Sam sometimes whistles softly as he works, but mostly he just thinks about what he is doing.

Freddie wears baggy coveralls with lots of large pockets. He stuffs them with nails and tools and extra snacks. But his nails are often in the pocket where he thought he had his raisins. And he finds that the hammer loop is a handy place to hang a banana.

Sam and Freddie are building this house for Mr. and Mrs. Best, who want it all just perfect.

They own a nice building lot, and they had their
plans for a house neatly drawn up. Mr. Best
called the Whackytack Construction Company
because he'd seen the name on Sam's truck and
thought it was funny. Mrs. Best wasn't sure she
wanted a funny company to build her house,
but she liked Sam and Freddie. So the carpenter
put up a sign that read The Best House and
started building on the lot.

Soon the outside walls were up, and the roof was on. Mr. Drain, the plumber, finished all the pipes. Mr. Sparks, the electrician, strung all the wires.

One day when he was looking at the plans, Freddie decided that the inside of the house was boring. The more he thought about it, the more ideas he thought of to improve things. Sam came in just as Freddie was about to cut a round hole in the ceiling.

"What are you doing?" Sam yelled. "The chimney doesn't go there!"

"Oh, this isn't the chimney," said Freddie. "This is a hole for a fire fighter's pole. Stairs take up too much room. A pole is more fun—and faster, too!"

"Faster coming down, maybe," said Sam. "But how about going back up? Somehow I can't see Mrs. Best shinnying up a pole in a silk dress and high heels."

"Well-l-l-l," said Freddie, "we could put a ladder leaning on the side of the hole."

Sam shook his head.

"Okay," Freddie sighed, "stairs, then. But at least let's put in a wide banister so that Mr. and Mrs. Best can slide down when they want to."

The next day Freddie was standing in the dining room. He looked out the east window at the apple trees in bloom. He looked out the south window to the faraway hills. Then he took out his chalk and drew a big circle on the floor.

Sam came into the room. "What is that for?" he asked.

"Well, I was thinking." Freddie put his finger on his chin. "Both these windows have pretty views. But a person looking out one can't see the other. Now if the table and chairs were on a big merry-go-round, then a motor could turn it slowly and each person could see everything!"

Sam shook his head. "Somehow, Freddie, I don't think Mr. and Mrs. Best are going to go for that idea. Suppose Mr. Best were carrying in a

big plate of biscuits. He'd have to jump on the merry-go-round, and biscuits would go flying all over."

Freddie had to agree, but he hated to give up his idea. "We could just have the table go around, and then no one would ever have to pass anything."

Sam shook his head again. "Let's stick to the plans, Freddie. The house doesn't belong to us."

But Freddie kept wanting to do something to make the house more fun. By now he knew it had to be a secret that neither Sam nor the Bests would notice for a while. A little funny secret that just Freddie knew about.

Then he had the idea! He did it when Sam went down to the hardware store for more cupboard latches. Mr. and Mrs. Best didn't see it until they moved in. Nobody knew except Freddie.

But when Mr. Best carried a box of old books up to the attic, there it was. A swing! A lovely, old-fashioned swing with smooth, thick rope hanging from a heavy beam at the top of the house. Its seat was made from a piece of wood stained and varnished like furniture. Carefully carved underneath were the words *Freddie Was Here*.

Sometimes Mr. Best sneaks up the attic stairs, sits in the swing, and looks out the window at the apple trees. He remembers what fun it was to play when he was young. He smiles, swings a little, and feels happy.

Sometimes Mrs. Best does that, too. And they both recommend the Whackytack Construction Company to all their friends.

Pamela's Parrot

By Betty Bates

Pamela's parrot was named Fitch. Fitch had gray and white and red and black feathers and a large black bill. Sometimes he sat on the perch in his cage in the living room and admired himself in his mirror. Sometimes he chewed on his seeds and fruit. Sometimes he watched Pamela playing with her fire engine. But most of all he liked to repeat what people said.

If Pamela said, "Stop talking and eat your banana," Fitch would say, "Stop talking and eat your banana." Pamela's dad said, "Parrots never know what the words mean. They only imitate people."

One afternoon Mrs. Grigsby came to collect money for the hospital charity fund. After Pamela's mom gave her a check, Mrs. Grigsby kept sitting as if she were stuck to her chair.

Pamela hoped she would go home soon, so she and her mom could finish their checker game. But Mrs. Grigsby talked and talked.

"Stop talking and eat your banana," said Fitch.

"Well, I never!" Mrs. Grigsby exclaimed. She got up and swished out of the house.

"Oh dear," said Pamela's mom. "Fitch has upset Mrs. Grigsby."

"Serves her right," muttered Pamela to herself.

"It's not polite to mumble," said her mom.

The next afternoon Gus, the repair person, came to fix the TV in the living room. He grinned at Pamela, who was playing with her fire engine. "Howareyoutoday?" he said.

Pamela thought Gus had asked, "How are you today?" so she answered, "I'm fine."

Gus spread parts all over the top of the TV set. "I'llhavethisfixedinnotime," he said.

"It's not polite to mumble," said Fitch.

"Well, I never!" said Gus. He gathered up his tools and left, without even stopping to say good-bye.

"Oh dear," said Pamela's mom when she saw the parts scattered on the television set. "We'll never get the TV fixed."

The next morning, after Pamela's family listened to the Radio Roy call-in talk show at breakfast, Pamela's dad left for work. "Shut the door behind you when you leave," called out Pamela's mom.

That afternoon Pamela's cousin Carey brought her guitar to try out a new song, "The Bad News Blues," on Pamela and her mom. It was long and gloomy. When Carey had finished, Pamela's mom cleared her throat and said, "Hmmm."

"Shut the door behind you when you leave," said Fitch.

"Well, I never!" Carey said. She left immediately, shutting the door behind her.

"Oh dear," said Pamela's mom. "Fitch has hurt her feelings. Pamela, we're going to have to get rid of Fitch."

"Oh, no!" said Pamela. "Give him time. I'll try to get Fitch to behave."

"All right," said her mom. "He can have one week."

Pamela tried hard to keep Fitch from talking. She kept saying "Shhh!" but Fitch didn't seem to understand what "Shhh" meant. During that week Fitch insulted the mail carrier, the meter reader, and the parcel delivery person. When Pamela's dad came home for dinner at the end of the week, her mom said, "Fitch has to go."

"How come?" asked Pamela's dad.

"Because," said Pamela's mom, "last week he was rude to Mrs. Grigsby, Carey, and Gus, who left parts all over the TV set. And this week he insulted the mail carrier, the meter reader, and the parcel delivery person."

"Well, well," said Pamela's dad. "We'll have to get rid of Fitch, all right."

"It's not Fitch's fault!" cried Pamela. "You said that parrots only imitate. They never know what the words mean."

"You're right, Pamela. I did say that."

"If only we could let people know that," said her mom.

"Why can't we?" asked Pamela. She thought for a minute. "I've got it. I'll call Radio Roy. I'll tell him Fitch isn't responsible for what he says."

"Not a bad idea," said her dad.

"Everyone in town listens to the Radio Roy show," said her mom.

The next morning Pamela called the station and explained her problem to Radio Roy. "I've got a parrot named Fitch who makes remarks he doesn't mean. He's hurt a lot of feelings lately.

So I want everybody to know that Fitch isn't responsible for what he says. He just repeats things he's heard—at all the wrong times."

"I get the picture," said Radio Roy. "I hope all those people are listening, Pamela. Hey, thanks for calling."

After lunch that day the mail carrier, the meter reader, and the parcel delivery person all dropped over to say they had no hard feelings. Gus turned up, grinning. "I came to fix the television set," he said, speaking clearly. Mrs. Grigsby came too. She sat with the others and listened respectfully to Carey, who played a new song called "Get Lost, Baby." The tune had a catchy beat that set people tapping their toes.

Pamela and her mom served snacks, and Pamela's dad passed around soft drinks. All their guests were chattering happily when a gravelly voice cut in. "Get lost, baby."

It was Fitch.

Everyone smiled.

Pamela smiled with them. She wasn't worried, because she knew—now everyone knew—that Fitch wasn't responsible for what he said.

But when she looked at Fitch, he winked at her.

So Pamela winked back.

The Legend of Pumpkin Hollow

By Laura Mellen

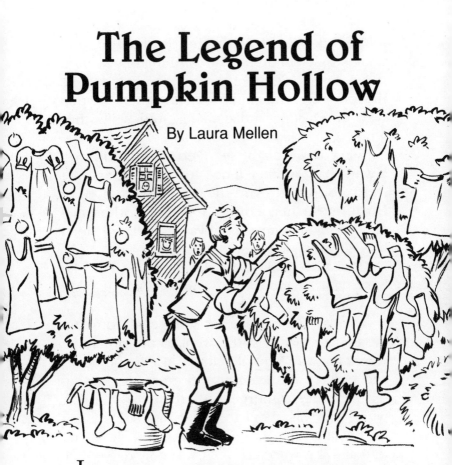

If you ever go over to Pumpkin Hollow, look up Mr. Bronson, who runs the general store. He can tell you the whole wonderful story of George Birthington and the great thing he did.

Mr. Bronson says that over a hundred years ago George Birthington lived on a farm near

Rattlesnake Creek with Mrs. Birthington and their seven children. The Birthingtons were a happy family. Some of the children helped with the plowing and milking. The others helped with the dusting and cooking. And while they worked, they laughed and sang.

Everyone was busy. George Birthington always had another fence to mend or another field to plant. And it seemed as if Mrs. Birthington just couldn't make clothes fast enough. Someone was always saying, "I don't have anything left to wear."

Almost every day Mrs. Birthington would be busy with her needle, sewing a dress or a shirt or whatever was needed.

One day George needed some cloth to tie up the tomato plants, so he went to the storeroom where his wife kept old clothes. He found boxes and baskets and even an old trunk overflowing with clothes. George pulled out something white. He was about to tear it into strips when he saw that it was his favorite shirt. It wasn't torn and it wasn't shabby. It was only dirty.

George took the shirt to his wife. "This was in with the old clothes by mistake," he said. "Will you wash it for me, please?"

Mrs. Birthington looked sad. "I can't wash it, George."

"Why not?" George asked.

"Because the washtub is full of geraniums!"

"Leave everything to me," George said. He planted the geraniums in the flower bed. Then he filled the tub with water and called to his wife, "You can wash the shirt now."

Mrs. Birthington dipped her little finger in the water and drew circles. "I'm sorry, George. I just can't do it."

George clapped his hand to his forehead. "Of course not, dearie. I forgot the soap. Here it is."

Mrs. Birthington looked at the soap, and she looked at George, and a tear rolled down her cheek. "You don't understand," she said. "I can't wash your shirt because I don't know how. I know how to cook, and I know how to sweep, and I'm very good at sewing. But I never learned how to wash clothes."

George patted his wife on the shoulder. "Don't cry, my dear. I'll wash the shirt myself."

When he was finished, George held the shirt up to show his wife. Mrs. Birthington was delighted. "It looks like new," she said. "I'm glad I won't have to make you another just yet. I'm tired of sewing all the time!"

George Birthington's face lit up with a good idea. "I know how to help you," he said to his wife. "Maybe you won't have to sew for months."

George went to the storeroom and picked up

an armload of clothes—some red, some green, some yellow. Then he returned for some pink and blue and white things. He washed them all and took them to the yard to dry. He hung the shirts on the lilac bush and the dresses on the branches of the apple tree. He carefully spread the handkerchiefs out on the grass. And he draped the socks all around the mulberry bush.

When Mrs. Jones went by, she thought the Birthingtons' yard looked like a giant flower garden. She hurried home to get her husband. "The Birthingtons must be having a party," she told him. "Come see the decorations."

"I love a party!" Mr. Jones said. "I'll take this cake I just baked."

Along the way other neighbors joined the Joneses. When they came to the Birthingtons' house, they all sat down in the yard to admire the beautiful sight. Someone started to clap, and they all took up the beat. When the Birthingtons came to see who was there, a cheer went up.

"You did a great thing, George!" Mr. Jones said.

"I did only what anyone would have done," George said. But you could see he was pleased.

It was a lovely party. While the children played tag, the grown-ups sang their favorite songs. Mr. Jones passed his cake around, and the others served lemonade and popcorn. It was so much fun that for many years afterward they all got together on that same day to celebrate.

At this point in the story, Mr. Bronson hands his listener one of his calendars. "Birthington was a great man," he says. "Did you know there is now a holiday in his honor?"

When you admit you didn't know, he turns to April on the calendar.

There it is, all right. Under April—April 1 to be exact—*George Birthington's Washday*.

APRIL FOOL!

Francis Milliken Minds His Manners

By Joyce Durham Barrett

When Francis Milliken left for his first day at school, his mother was full of instructions.

"Remember to say 'thank you' and 'please.' Try not to bother your classmates. You should do what the teacher says. And don't forget to mind your manners, dear."

Francis Milliken's mother was proud of her son. She had taken great care to teach him the proper way to talk, to act, and to eat. She sucked in a deep breath, smiled, and said, "What a sweet little boy. The teacher will be so pleased with you, Francis Milliken."

Francis Milliken took great care to remember everything his mother had told him.

When the crossing guard blew her whistle for the students to cross the street, Francis Milliken marched right up to the officer and said quite properly, "I'll thank you to stop blowing that whistle so loud in my ears!"

Then Francis Milliken marched on to school, proud that he had remembered to say "thank you."

Francis Milliken also remembered to say "please." When all the lunch money had been collected, Miss King, the teacher, put the money into an envelope. She asked Lee Ann to take the money to the lunchroom.

"Young lady," said Francis Milliken, "please see that you don't dawdle along the way."

Francis Milliken sat up prim and straight in his desk, certain Miss King was impressed that he knew how to say "please."

Francis Milliken was especially glad that he knew not to bother his classmates.

When Tim collected the art papers, Francis

Milliken said, "Don't bother. I'll take my own paper to Miss King, thank you."

And when Amy passed out paper cups for juice during the morning break, Francis Milliken said, "Never mind, dear. I'll get my own paper cup, okay?"

When books or pencils dropped to the floor, he rushed to pick them up for his classmates. "Allow me," Francis Milliken said with a sweeping bow.

All the students looked with puzzlement at Francis Milliken. And the more they looked at him, the prouder he grew, for he knew that surely they must be admiring how polite he was.

When Miss King went to the teachers' lounge, Francis Milliken kept a sharp lookout around the room. Every time someone yawned and looked sleepy, he made a trumpet of his hands and yelled, "It's not nice to yawn when you have all this company around you!"

So Francis Milliken made sure that no one took a nap during naptime.

Next, it was time for music. Miss King brought out the box of rhythm instruments. Francis Milliken scrambled through the tambourines and maracas, jingle bells and wooden sticks. He pulled out a tambourine.

When the class marched to the music, Francis Milliken remembered what his mother always said: "If you're going to do something, do it with all your might."

So Francis Milliken marched with all his might. He lifted his knees so high they almost touched his chin. He sang so loud no one could hear the music. He hit his tambourine so hard he almost wore it out.

He almost wore out Miss King, too. Miss King looked the happiest of all when it came time to go to the playground. There Francis Milliken could run and scream until he used up all his energy.

But Francis Milliken didn't run and scream and use up all his energy. When he saw Miss King watching the pupils play, he felt sorry that she was all alone.

"Wouldn't you like some company?" Francis Milliken asked, sitting on the bench beside Miss King.

Miss King thought for a moment. "I've had a hard day, Francis Milliken," she said. "I think I'd really prefer being alone right now. Do you mind?"

Francis Milliken jumped up and shrugged. "Not at all," he said. "I know about hard days. I've had a hard day myself."

Miss King sighed. "What an unusual pupil you are, Francis Milliken. I believe you are the most unusual pupil that I have ever seen."

Francis Milliken ran off to play, with the teacher's words echoing in his ears.

That evening at dinner, Francis Milliken's mother asked about his manners. "And how did my sweet Francis do today? Did you remember to say 'please' and 'thank you'?" she asked.

Francis Milliken stuck his nose in the air as he tied his dinner napkin around his neck. "Yes, ma'am. All day long I said 'thank you' and 'please' and 'don't bother.' And do you know what? Miss King says I'm the most unusual pupil she's ever seen."

Francis Milliken's mother smiled. "My dear sweet Francis," she said, "what a joy you will be for Miss King this year."

A Simply Monstrous Time

By Linda Neves

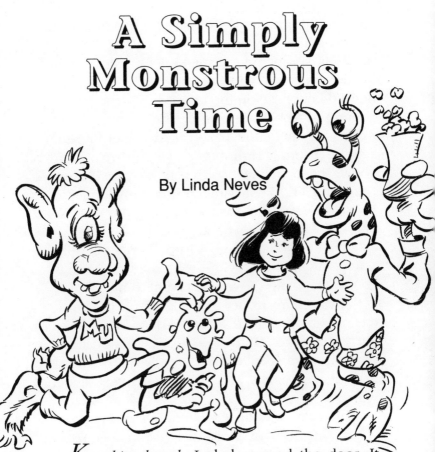

Knockitty-knock. Isobel opened the door. It was the neighborhood kids again.

"Isobel, Isobel, please come out and play," they sang. "It's a kite-flying, balloon-popping, watermelon day."

"Oh, no, I really couldn't," said little Isobel,

backing into the house. "I may get a phone call. My pet turtle may need to be fed. My avocado pit might sprout. My cat might get her tail caught in the door. It could rain, and what if it's too hot? I'd better stay in the house."

In truth, Isobel was terribly shy.

That day her Aunt Ezzy called Isobel into the sewing room. "Halloween is tomorrow, and you've been invited to a costume party," Aunt Ezzy told her. "You can dress as anything you want to be. No one will know you are shy. No one will even know you are you."

"I couldn't possibly go," Isobel replied hastily. "My goldfish might swim upside down, although he never has, and I wouldn't want to miss that."

But the more Isobel thought about that party, the more she wanted to go—just to see what a party was like. "If I dress up as a monster, I won't be afraid," she told herself. "I'll be furry, and I'll have fangs and sharp fingernails, and I won't be shy."

Aunt Ezzy was an excellent seamstress, and she was only too pleased to sew a monster costume. She stayed up almost all night, stitching a costume from old coats. Isobel tried to stay awake, but she fell asleep on a big scrap of furry cloth.

The next morning Isobel tried on her costume.

"Eeek!" shrieked Aunt Ezzy as she clasped her

hands to her heart. "You gave me quite a fright. I thought you were a real monster."

On Halloween night Aunt Ezzy gave Isobel directions to the party. It was only a few blocks away, so Isobel memorized the directions.

"Left here, right there, straight ahead," she sang to herself. As she swaggered down the street, Isobel didn't feel shy anymore. "Hello!" she called to the sidewalk. "Step aside," she said to a telephone pole.

Soon she saw some partygoers standing in a doorway, all dressed up as monsters. "This must be the place," she said. "Monster costumes sure are popular this year."

Isobel handed her coat to the butler at the door. Inside were monsters tall, short, fat, and skinny, and all of them were ugly. She saw green slime dripping from the ceiling, and she listened to music filled with howls and screeches.

Some monsters were dancing. Some munched purple popcorn. Now and then the lights went off, and everyone clapped for the monsters who glowed in the dark. Isobel danced the Monster Mash, the Terrible Two-Step, and the Werewolf Waltz. Her partners had scary costumes but friendly smiles.

After the party games, there was a contest to see who had the best costume. The monsters formed a line and paraded around the room. Three judges jotted notes in their black books. When they finished, they cleared their throats.

"May we have your attention," they shouted. "Will number 23 please step forward?" No one came. "Number 23," repeated the judges. "Number 23 is the winner."

Isobel looked at her number. Number 23! It couldn't be, but it was. She ran to the judges, and they pinned a Miss Monster ribbon on her fur. They gave her a big bouquet of wilted weeds and a crown that looked like melted cheese.

"I love it!" Isobel exclaimed. "Thank you." Everyone clapped their hands and wagged their tails.

"Now we'll take off our costumes," said the judges. Off came the fangs and fake fingernails, the warts and the wigs, the jewelry and the furs. Isobel looked around the room and gasped.

"Oh my goodness," she said. "Even without their costumes, these monsters are real monsters! I must have come to the wrong party!"

But Isobel was having too much fun to care. She took off her feathers and her fur and her mask, and pretended she was really a monster, too.

All too soon, the monsters began saying their good-byes. "It was a simply smashing bash," said a pink bubble monster.

"I had a simply monstrous time," Isobel told him. He giggled, showing her his fangs.

Aunt Ezzy was waiting up when Isobel got home.

"I had a ghastly good time," said Isobel. "And I won first prize for the costume you made!"

Isobel fell asleep as soon as her head hit the pillow. She dreamed of friendly monsters hiding in the yard, eating cream puffs and telling jokes.

After breakfast the next morning Isobel heard a knock at the door. "I'll get it," she called. It was the neighborhood kids again.

"Isobel, Isobel, please come out and play," they sang.

"Why, I'd love to," Isobel said softly, before they could sing the next line. "I'd simply love to come out and play."

And Isobel stepped out into the sunshine.

The Backward Runner

By Elaine Wilson

It seems most of the guys I know have something they like to do whenever they get the chance . . . like shooting baskets or shuffling cards.

I've got something I like to do, too. I don't expect to get famous or anything, but it is what I do whenever I get the chance. I like to run backward.

I can't remember how I got started running backward, except all of a sudden one day I just realized that was what I did whenever I could. So right then I started working on it. It's not really all that easy to do, you know. I mean, I've tripped over rocks and crashed into trees, and once I dropped into a ditch some guy was digging. But that's all part of the challenge of it.

A backward runner has really got to have good ears. I mean, you've got to listen for all sorts of noises . . . like little kids riding tricycles and older people sweeping sidewalks.

Just lately I've started working on carrying things while I run. I ran home backward from the store the other day with a whole bag of groceries for my mother. Last week, I looked at a book while I was running home from the library.

I'm trying to build up my speed, too. I've started timing myself when I run home from school and when I come home from my job at the theater.

I've got this sort-of job, you see. I say "sort-of" because I don't get paid money, and it's kind of my hobby anyway. I help Mrs. Wheeler sweep up her movie theater after the shows are over. For that, Mrs. Wheeler lets me in free to see all the movies that are okay for twelve-year-old kids to see. And I get to eat all the popcorn and candy I want . . . as long as I don't eat too much.

I really get a kick out of seeing the same movie a couple of times. I always sit clear down front, so I feel as if I'm in the action. Just the other night I was watching this movie I'd seen only five times. The part I liked best was just

coming—it's the part where the monster gets into the elevator full of people—when I noticed I was almost out of popcorn. I didn't want to miss my favorite part. So I figured the quickest way to get more popcorn and see the movie at the same time was . . . you guessed it . . . to run up the aisle backward. I stepped out into the aisle and began to put my feet in reverse.

That's just about all I remember . . . except for a loud screech. The next thing I knew I was lying on the floor, staring up at the lights on the ceiling.

They tell me that just as I started my run, Mrs. Mook got up to leave the movie. When she saw me coming, she screamed and whammed me with her purse. That must have been what stopped me.

With all that confusion, Mrs. Wheeler shut down the projector and turned on the lights to check things out.

Mrs. Mook stuck around long enough to see that I was still breathing, and then she stormed out of the theater mumbling something about never knowing what's going to happen next.

Mrs. Wheeler helped me to my feet and asked, "Are you okay, Robert?"

"Yes," I said. "Just got a sore spot on my head, that's all."

She walked me to the lobby. I figured she was really going to let me have it. To my surprise, she said, "I don't think Mrs. Mook meant to hurt you. You just scared her. But I do think that none of this would have happened if you hadn't been running backward up the aisle. I would appreciate it if you wouldn't run anymore in the theater . . . either frontward or backward."

"I won't, ma'am," I said. I used "ma'am" so she would know I was really serious.

Then she said, "Now why don't you go home? I'll sweep up tonight and see you here tomorrow evening."

"Thanks," I said. "See you tomorrow."

I walked home. My head hurt a little bit, and I wanted to do some thinking. I was sure glad I hadn't lost my sort-of job. You know, ever since I've known my mother, she has been saying things that sound as if she read them somewhere. It's crazy . . . they pop into my head at the weirdest times. As I was walking home, one of Mom's sayings did just that.

"There's a time and place for everything."

I figure I finally understand what that one means.